# Dear Parents:

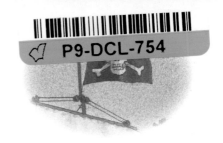

Congratulations! Your child is taking the first steps on an exciting journey. The destination? Independent reading!

**STEP INTO READING®** will help your child get there. The program offers five steps to reading success. Each step includes fun stories and colorful art or photographs. In addition to original fiction and books with favorite characters, there are Step into Reading Non-Fiction Readers, Phonics Readers and Boxed Sets, Sticker Readers, and Comic Readers—a complete literacy program with something to interest every child.

## Learning to Read, Step by Step!

**Ready to Read    Preschool–Kindergarten**
• big type and easy words • rhyme and rhythm • picture clues
For children who know the alphabet and are eager to begin reading.

**Reading with Help    Preschool–Grade 1**
• basic vocabulary • short sentences • simple stories
For children who recognize familiar words and sound out new words with help.

**Reading on Your Own    Grades 1–3**
• engaging characters • easy-to-follow plots • popular topics
For children who are ready to read on their own.

**Reading Paragraphs    Grades 2–3**
• challenging vocabulary • short paragraphs • exciting stories
For newly independent readers who read simple sentences with confidence.

**Ready for Chapters    Grades 2–4**
• chapters • longer paragraphs • full-color art
For children who want to take the plunge into chapter books but still like colorful pictures.

**STEP INTO READING®** is designed to give every child a successful reading experience. The grade levels are only guides; children will progress through the steps at their own speed, developing confidence in their reading.

Remember, a lifetime love of reading starts with a single step!

Thomas the Tank Engine & Friends™

CREATED BY BRITT ALLCROFT

Based on The Railway Series by The Reverend W Awdry.
© 2020, 2015 Gullane (Thomas) LLC.
Thomas the Tank Engine & Friends and Thomas & Friends are trademarks of Gullane (Thomas) Limited.
© HIT Entertainment Limited. HIT and the HIT logo are trademarks of HIT Entertainment Limited.

Visit us on the Web!
StepIntoReading.com
rhcbooks.com
www.thomasandfriends.com

Educators and librarians, for a variety of teaching tools, visit us at RHTeachersLibrarians.com

ISBN 978-0-553-52171-9 (trade)

Printed in the United States of America
16 15 14 13 12 11 10 9 8 7

HiT entertainment

STEP INTO READING®

STEP 1 READY TO READ

THOMAS & FRIENDS™

# THE LOST SHIP

Based on The Railway Series
by The Reverend W Awdry

Illustrated by Richard Courtney

Random House 🏠 New York

The sun comes up.

# Time for work!

But Thomas does not
want to work.

# He wants to race!

# Crash!

Down, down, down
he falls.

Thomas lands next to
a lost pirate ship!

# Thomas meets Sailor John and his boat, Skiff.

# They are looking for treasure!

The sailor has a map.

X marks the spot!

They look and look.
They do not find it.

# Marion finds the treasure!

It will go in a museum.

The sailor is angry.

He steals the chest
that night!

Skiff and Thomas
try to stop him.

The chest is heavy.

Skiff starts to sink!

The sailor has
to let the treasure go.

# Splash!

Down, down, down
it falls.

The police take
Sailor John away.

The treasure is lost.
But not for long!

Divers haul it up
from the deep.

# The treasure finds
# a new home.

# Skiff finds a new job!

Thomas is as happy
as can be.